Dedication ...

to *Kamau,*
my precious miracle

to *Reg*
for your constant love

Every morning Neeko prayed that he wouldn't have to go to school. "But Lord, if I *do* have to go to school, please, don't let me see Kyle Thomas. But if I *do* have to see Kyle, please Lord, don't let Kyle see me. But if Kyle *does* see me, please don't let him talk about me."

But every morning, Neeko would walk into his classroom and see Kyle sitting there. First, Kyle would grin at him. Then Kyle would let him have it! Neeko could tell that this morning was going to be just like all the others. "Looks like you wore your best clothes today!" Kyle yelled. Kyle's friends whispered and laughed.

Neeko looked down. His jeans were a little too tight and a little too short. His t-shirt was faded. His shoes were worn. Neeko's mother bought him the best clothes she could afford, but they were never as nice as the other kids' clothes.

Even though he was angry and ashamed, Neeko kept his mouth shut. But Kyle wouldn't stop. "Hey Neeko! I've got some clothes at home that my mom is throwing out. Do you want to come look through our trash for something to wear tomorrow?"

That did it. Neeko raced out of the class and all the way to the bathroom before his tears started to fall. He was angry at Kyle, but he was even angrier that the same thing happened every morning, even if he prayed.

"Hey, Neeko."

The voice sounded familiar, but Neeko was scared. Maybe he was in trouble for leaving class.

"Neeko, come out."

Neeko opened the door of the stall and saw a face he knew. It was his friend, Troy. No one else knew about Troy because he only visited Neeko when he was alone, and usually just when Neeko needed help or was feeling really unhappy.

Neeko was feeling pretty unhappy right now. "What's up, Troy?"

"Somebody told me you need some extra help getting through this day," said Troy.

Neeko's words came rushing out. "I don't think I can make it. Even before class started Kyle had all those kids laughing at me. Every morning I pray and it doesn't do any good. I just want to go home and never come back."

Troy looked into Neeko's eyes. "God hears your prayers, Neeko. Sometimes we just don't get the answer we want because God wants us to learn something from what we're going through."

That made Neeko angry again. "What can I learn from being laughed at all day?"

"Well, whatever you're supposed to learn, you won't learn it in the bathroom," said Troy. "Just remember that I'll be looking out for you. I've got your back, Neeko."

And just like that, Troy was gone. When Neeko returned to class, his teacher, Mr. Blackstone, could see Neeko was upset, so Neeko didn't get in trouble for missing the first minutes of class. Somehow, Neeko made it through the rest of the day. Just knowing that Troy was looking out for him made things easier to handle. As Neeko was leaving to go home, Mr. Blackstone handed him an envelope. "Neeko, your work this year has been so good that you've won a special award. Give this note to your mother. It's her invitation to the awards assembly." "Thanks, Mr. Blackstone! I won't forget!"

Suddenly, Neeko's day was looking much better.

When his mom came home from work, Neeko gave her the envelope right away. He knew that his hard work in school made his mom very happy. But she sure didn't look happy as she read the note inside.

"This says you can't read!" she cried, looking confused. Neeko's mouth fell open. What happened to his award? "But that's impossible," his mother continued. "You've been reading to me since you were five years old!"

As she finished reading the note, Neeko's mom breathed a sigh of relief. "Oh Neeko, there's been a mistake. This note isn't for you. It's got another boy's name here at the bottom." She put the note back in the envelope and stuck it in Neeko's backpack. "Give this back to Mr. Blackstone tomorrow, but don't read it. Only the other boy's parents should read that note."

Now Neeko usually did what his mother told him to do, but he just couldn't resist looking at that note. As he waited for the school bus the next morning, Neeko opened his backpack and took out the envelope. He unfolded the note and read it quickly. It said that the student was having trouble because he couldn't read. When Neeko looked at the bottom of the note and saw the name written there, he gasped.

"He can't read!" Neeko laughed. "Kyle can't read! Now I can get him back for all the mean things he's said about me." Neeko closed his eyes and imagined it. He was smiling and laughing to himself when he heard a quiet voice.

"Hey, Neeko." Neeko opened his eyes. It was Troy again.

"Hey, Troy!" Neeko yelled.

"What's making you so happy?" Troy asked.

Neeko was so excited that his words came out in a rush. "Troy, I found something.
A note was supposed to go to Kyle's parents, but Mr. Blackstone gave it to me by
mistake. And guess what? Kyle can't read! I finally have something to say back to
Kyle! He won't be able to make fun of me anymore! You told me that my prayers
would work!"

Troy smiled, but then he asked, "Neeko, how do you feel when Kyle talks about
you?"

"Embarassed. You know that." Neeko was starting to get upset with Troy.

"Does it make you feel worse that Kyle talks about things you can't change!" Troy
said quietly.

"Yes! That's why this is so perfect!   I can finally hurt Kyle the way he hurt me!
You're trying to change my mind!" Neeko yelled. He was angry now. He couldn't
believe that Troy wanted to take away his chance to get even.

Troy was quiet for a while. Finally, he said, "Neeko, remember when you told me that you prayed every morning but that Kyle still teased you anyway? Do you remember what I told you?"

Neeko nodded, but wouldn't answer.

"I think God wants you to learn something. God loves you and doesn't want you to be hurt and sad. But guess what? God loves Kyle too."

Neeko was so shocked, he blurted out, "But how could God love someone so bad?"

Troy smiled. "Neeko, even though God loves Kyle, He can't stand the fact that Kyle hurts people. Maybe this note is a way for you to stop hurting and for Kyle to stop hurting you." Neeko looked down at his feet. He couldn't believe what Troy was saying. He looked up to ask a question, but Troy was gone. Just then the bus pulled up.

Neeko didn't want to go to class now. He couldn't stand the thought of seeing Kyle and his friends. Not only would he have to listen to their teasing, but now that he had a way to fight back, he couldn't even use it! When Neeko got to his classroom door, he saw Kyle waiting for him. But Kyle wasn't smiling as usual.

"I have something for you," Kyle whispered to Neeko, handing him the note about the awards assembly. "Do you have something for me?" Kyle asked. His voice was shaking. Neeko couldn't believe it! Kyle actually looked scared!

"Yes," Neeko answered. "Here's your note."

"Did you read it?" Kyle asked.

"Yes. Look, I'm sorry."

Kyle stared at Neeko for a while before he looked down and spoke softly. "Please don't tell anybody. People will laugh at me if they know I can't read." Just then Neeko realized that he wasn't mad at Kyle anymore. Kyle looked just as scared and alone as Neeko looked whenever Kyle laughed at him. Neeko knew that he could hurt Kyle even worse than Kyle had hurt him. Suddenly, Neeko knew what God wanted him to do.

"Don't worry, Kyle. I won't tell your secret."

Kyle looked like he was going to cry. "Why? I talked about you and made the other guys laugh. Don't you want to get me back?"

Neeko knew that yesterday he wanted that more than anything. "Maybe now that you know how I feel, you can stop talking about me."

Kyle grinned. "You're right. Thanks for being so nice. From now on, we're friends, okay?"

Neeko grinned back at Kyle. "Okay."

Neeko walked into class, and Kyle followed him, smiling. Kyle's friends waited for him to joke about Neeko, but instead Kyle put an arm around Neeko's shoulders. Kyle's friends were shocked. They couldn't believe that Kyle would want to be Neeko's friend! After a while, though, Kyle's friends began to tell Neeko hello and act friendly toward him. Neeko thought that this was the best morning he could remember.

Later that evening, Troy came to see Neeko in his room.

"So, you didn't tell anybody that Kyle can't read, huh?" Troy smiled as he put his hand on Neeko's shoulder.

"No, I decided to do the right thing." Neeko was smiling too.

"So now you understand."

"Understand what?" Neeko was a little confused.

"You understand what kindness is. You understand that you should be kind, even when other people are mean to you."

"I guess so. Is that what God wanted me to learn this whole time?"

"I think so," said Troy. "I think He also wanted you to know that you should always listen to *me*!" Troy laughed and hugged Neeko. Neeko laughed and thought to himself that sometimes an angel is the best friend you can have.

About the Author

Melanie Mims is the author of *Not All Angels Have Wings*, as well as other works of short fiction and poetry. She resides in Marietta, GA with her husband and two sons.

About the Illustrator

John Floyd Jr. lives in Smyrna, GA. He owns John's Creative Art, a company that specializes in murals and Fine Art collectables. John's work has been exhibited in Galleries located in Georgia, New York and Alaska.

Photographs by Rose Mascotti